This book belongs to:
....

For bookworms, dreamers, and little kids with big imaginations!
Rosie

To my family, for all of their encouragement, love, and support.
Amariah

First published in the United Kingdom in 2021 by Lantana Publishing Ltd.
www.lantanapublishing.com | info@lantanapublishing.com

American edition published in 2021 by Lantana Publishing Ltd., UK.

A CIP catalogue record for this book is available from the British Library.

Distributed in the United States and Canada by Lerner Publishing Group, Inc.
241 First Avenue North, Minneapolis, MN 55401 U.S.A.
For reading levels and more information, look for this title at www.lernerbooks.com
Cataloging-in-Publication Data Available.

Printed and bound in China.
Original artwork using watercolor and charcoal, finished digitally.

Hardcover ISBN: 978-1-911373-97-1
Softcover ISBN: 978-1-911373-98-8
PDF ISBN: 978-1-911373-99-5
Trade ePub3 ISBN: 978-1-913747-64-0
S&L ePub3 ISBN: 978-1-913747-46-6

Sunday Rain

Rosie J. Pova
Amariah Rauscher

It started with a **WHOOSH** from the wind and a **KNOCK** from a branch weighing down on the window.

Elliott put down his book and peeked outside.

A leaf flew by, swinging down and side to side. Then another and another.

WHOOSH,

the wind whispered again.

Lightning zigzagged
through the clouds.

crashed thunder.

Elliott hopped back on his bed
and pulled his book onto his lap.

The princess was still fighting the dragon,
and the sea kept swallowing the royal boat as
the night pushed the day down the horizon.

Tap, Tap, pattered the raindrops on the roof.

Elliott turned the page.
That's when he heard laughter.
Elliott walked up to the window once more and glued his nose to the glass.

The storm had passed, and the kids from his street had gathered to play—skipping, springing, and splashing in oodles of puddles.

Elliott stood at the window, staring. Someone looked up. Elliott stepped back.

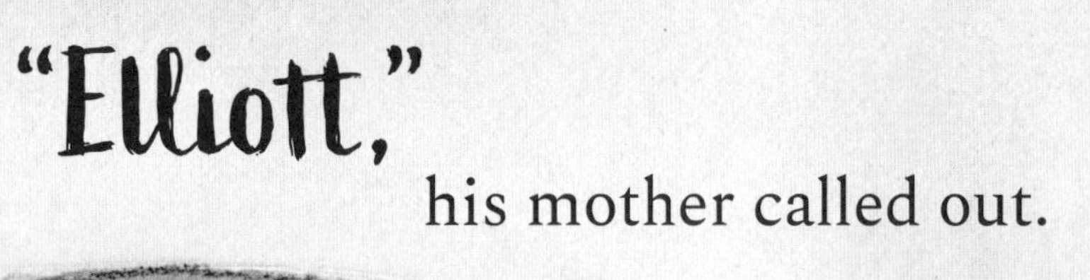

"Elliott," his mother called out.

He tucked the book under his pillow and ran downstairs.

“Sunday rain is the most fun,” Mama said.
“I bet your Sharkies are begging for a splash.”

Elliott thought for a moment.
“Go on,” Mama nudged. “Make some friends while I finish unpacking.”

Outside smelled like wet grass and flowers and the pages of a new book. Elliott looked around. He hesitated. But then . . .

ROOAAAR!

Elliott took a deep breath.

STOMP!

He jumped on one foot.

"My boat is filling up with water," he said to no one in particular.

"Row faster!"
someone replied.
"The island is near."

“The dragon is pushing me,” Elliott said.
“We’ll fight it,” someone else replied.

"PULL! PULL! PULL!"

all the kids shouted as they tugged the dragon's tail.

"We made it to the island!"
Elliott somersaulted in victory.

S.S. Elliott

WHOOSH, blew the wind, sprinkling raindrops from the branches above. Elliott caught a few on his tongue.

A sunray sparkled through a crack in the clouds. Then another and another.

Inside, the house smelled like freshly
baked bread and stew and warmth.
It was time for supper.

Up in his room, Elliott curled up with his book again. The princess befriended the dragon and saved the kingdom.

HOO-HOOO, hooted an owl outside the window.
Elliott hugged his book and drifted off to sleep.